The Has Beans© Work It Out

By Kari Grace

DEDICATION

This is dedicated to the Lover of my soul,
the One who saw worth and value in me
when I saw nothing but shame,
the One who chose to
put breath in my body at birth
when I was born dead.
Thank you for all You have
done for me, and for
everything You have given me.
I live to praise You.

ACKNOWLEDGEMENTS

Without my dearest darling man, Wolf, and my two
sweet angels
Alee and Sara, there would be little depth to
anything I do. They
have taught me about love in the hard places,
regardless of cost.
They have taught me what it means to live my faith.
I also thank God for our three canine babies - Rock,
Little Bear, and Sasha – who, by entering my life,
have also taught me much about love.

As with all her stories, this tale contains no foul
language or sex scenes.
Should you find biblical principles and scripture
references more offensive than sex and profanity, this
might not be the book for you.

CrossEffective Publishing, llc©   copyright 2000
        All rights reserved

The Has Beans were at it again.
Every day seemed to end in a heated discussion and Beanadette had no idea why.
On days like this it was easy to give up on a relationship, but Bearnado was clueless.
Which hurt Beanadette deeply.
He kept blowing her off and ignoring her concerns.
With Beanardo always angry lately, Beanland was no longer her safe place.
Little spats were turning into bigger fights.
This is not the life she wanted, for herself or her bean.

"You say you care but you won't even spend time with me any more," she said gently one Sunday afternoon as they walked through Beanstalk Gardens enjoying the sunshine.

He let go of her hand.

"There's no time. I have to work so hard, and I'm always tired. It's hard to stay at the Bean Counter Fiduciary Bank year after year with no appreciation. No bean ever says anything good."

He huffed loudly.

"I encourage you all the time!"

She turned sad eyes toward him.

He frowned, shrugged, and stalked off.

"You're such a podlicker!" she said in frustration. Beanadette wasn't getting through; she needed a way to connect where Beanardo would understand. She loved him deeply but she couldn't keep trusting him with her heart when he kept breaking it with his hurtful words.

She wasn't sure how much she could take, but she knew who to talk to about it.

She knelt down right there in the garden and whispered the only words she could think of. "Lord, help."

A gentle breeze swept through the daisies as if in answer to her prayer, and she felt a sense of peace as she started for home.

She smiled at the sunflowers when they came in view.

They never failed to put her in a good mood.

It was a wonderful day to be a bean in Beanland.

Even if Beanardo couldn't see it right now.

He had become the most negative bean in the world sometimes.

She for one refused to do the same.

It resulted in nothing but pain.

She should know.

When Beanardo got home he was mad as a bean could possibly be without cracking his skin.

Why was Beanadette always on his case?

He did all he could to make her happy.

He worked his beanpods to the bone all the hours God gave him. What more did she want?

He threw himself angrily onto the couch and grabbed the remote.

Maybe some time watching the bean box would help his mood improve.

The Has Beans 𝄀

When Beanadette got home she went straight to her prayer chair and started talking to God about Beanardo.

She started off upset, asking God why he got so defensive all the time. She poured out her wounded heart to the One who created her and loved her with an everlasting love.

A soft answer came to her heart.

"He doesn't know how to trust."

"OK, Lord, how can I help?"

"Kindness and patience are a great start," she felt Him whisper.

"I can do that," she said, and got out her notebook. Now she had a goal. She just had to figure out a plan.

After two solid hours of watching Beandy Gruffuth reruns Beanardo didn't feel any better.

In fact he felt worse.

He wouldn't admit it to anybean but he knew the bean box never helped. Not really.

It was like a drug. Beans everywhere used it to distract them from their real life problems while they stuffed unmet needs deep down inside.

He should know. His mother was an Addict.

Everybean tried to help but she was beyond saving. Her brain turned to mush as she sat watching the bean box day and night, not eating, not sleeping, not caring.

Eventually she withered away to nothing.

And he was left abandoned and alone when he was only a small sprout.

Which is why he knew there was no bean he could trust. Ever.

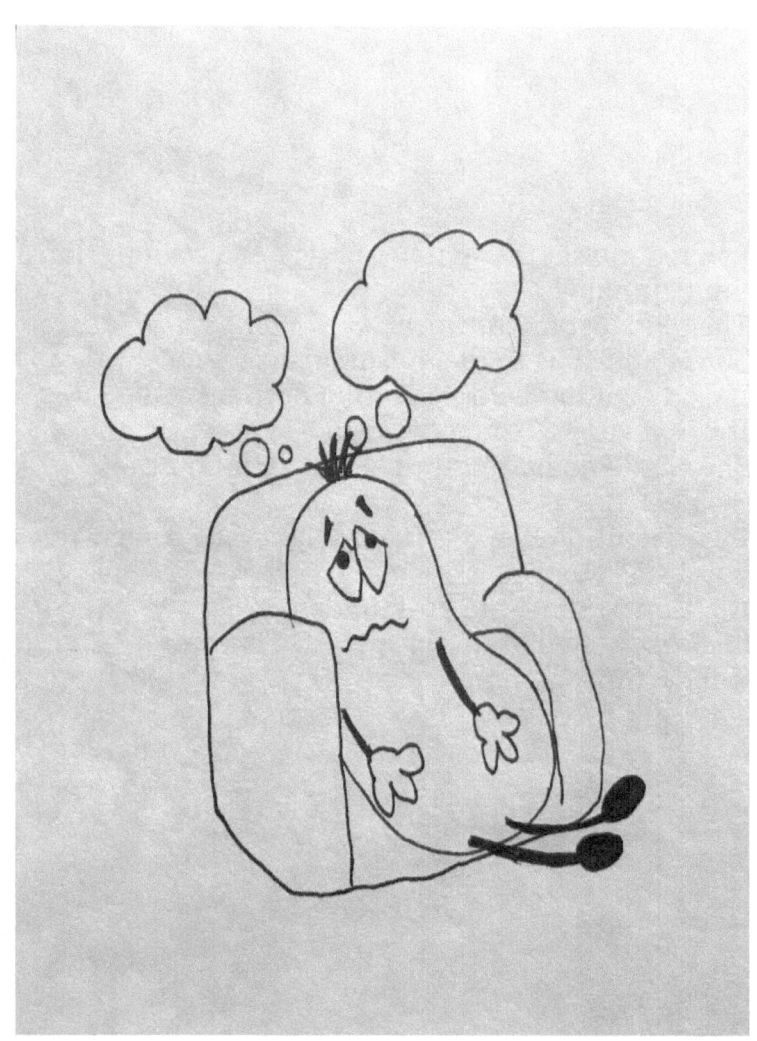

Beanadette sat there in her prayer chair a long, long time, thinking.

The plan just might work.

She would start in the morning, take it day by day.

If God couldn't help Beanardo, nothing could.

It was all up to Him, now.

She would do her part, then trust Him for the results.

Implementing Plan Patience might take some work but it was doable.

And she was just the bean to do it.

She cared enough to try, at least. That was a wonderful beginning.

Love proves itself in the hard places.

Beanardo believed this in theory, but he'd never really experienced it in his own short life.

Growing up as an orphan bean nobean gives a root about, you're just one of a sea of nameless shoots in the way of other beans with purpose and passion and plans for the day.

When you end up with no stalk to call your own, and even your own mother doesn't think you worth caring about...

yeah, it really does a number on a bean's self-esteem, especially at such an early age.

No wonder he had trust issues!

"There has to be more to life than this!" he growled as he heated up some left-over leaf stew for dinner.

Beanadette got up bright and early the very next day, excited to put Plan Patience into action.
The first step in her plan involved food.
Bearnardo ate like a weed and was always interested in free food.
Of course, to get it he would have to spend time with her, and hopefully talk.
She wasn't sure how much he would open up but a bean never knows till they try, right?
She was ready to try.
Tonight seemed as good a time as any to start Phase One.

Beanardo was getting ready to leave for work when he heard a letter fall through the mail slot in his stalk door.

"Guess Beanstorm is delivering early today," he mused thoughtfully as he grabbed his lunch and jacket and headed out of the door.

He bent down to pick up the envelope.

It was from Beanadette.

He huffed in an irritated way.

"What does she want now?" he groused as he slammed the front door. Hard.

The Has Beans 🌙

Beanadette hummed softly to herself as she set out for work that morning.

What a nice surprise it would be for Beanado when he came home to find an invitation to dinner waiting for him.

She walked briskly to the Beandays Café, hoping this small kindness would make a difference.

Things simply could not continue as they were.

She would not let that happen.

Something had to change.

And she was willing to take the first step.

Bearnado got work with two minutes to spare,
which made his boss hotter than a stray shoot.
He had to admit he didn't feel one bit bad.
Mr. Beanpole was a mean bean and a total piece of
work. He couldn't keep his eyes off the girls and he
was married, for bean patch sake!
Of course, that Beanice was a looker.
But he loved Beanadette.
Didn't he?
He started counting yesterday's beans and smiled at
the customers who walked by, but his mind was
elsewhere.

Beanadette was having a very busy day at the Beandays Café.

The weather had been sunny lately and everybean wanted to take advantage of the amazing coffee beans that grew this side of Beanpass Pass.

Which was fine with her. She loved hard work.

At lunch she sat at a spare table with her sandwich and water, watching the beans passing by. She knew most of them.

She nodded at old Mr. Beaner as he made his way slowly down Main Street.

He smiled a great big smile that crinkled his old beany face. She smiled back.

Beanice kept trying to talk but Beanardo didn't even notice.

He was so busy he didn't have time to read the letter until lunch.

It was short, and kind; Beanardo felt bad about being mean to her.

He was truly a podlicker. Of the worst kind.

She had asked him over for dinner tonight, and she was cooking his favorite.

Mean Green Bean Peas.

He sat and talked to God for a long time.

He knew his attitude was hurting her.

He wanted to change. He just didn't know how.

Then he had an idea. A terrific wonderful excellent idea.

He would stop by Mr. Beaner's house on the way home.

That bean had bean married for ever; if anybean knew what to do, it would be him.

"Well, young sproutster," said Mr. Beaner after Beanardo had explained his dilemma,
"... it sounds like you've got yourself in a right pickle. If I were you I'd sit down a spell and talk to the girl."
He called everybean 'sproutster', but it still made Beanardo smile.
The old guy had a way of getting you to like him.
There wasn't one bean in Beanland that didn't.
"But sir," he protested, "I don't even know where to begin. I've hurt her so badly."
"Start somewhere, young bean, but start. Tell her how you feel. Maybe it won't fix things but at least she'll know what's going on."
Mr. Beaner took a long sip of his bean tip tea and leaned forward.
"I wouldn't steer you wrong, sproutster. Be honest. It'll work out. I promise."

Beanadette hurried home from the Beandays Café and started dinner. Why he loved Mean Green Bean Peas was beyond her, but tonight was all about him. It was her first act of love as part of the Patience Plan.

She had run it by Momma B on the way home and Momma B gave it a two thumbs up, so perhaps she was on to something after all, however crazy it seemed.

After all, God is the only One who would tell somebean to be kind to a mean bean. Which is what Beanardo had become.

She still thought he could change. He just had to want to.

The Has Beans ◗

He arrived on time and he'd dressed up a little, to show her she was important to him.
As he knocked on the door he could smell her dinner and his mouth started to water.
Then it hit him.
She didn't like Mean Green Bean Peas.
She liked Beanpass Pasta.
She was doing this just for him.
When he had been so hurtful to her just yesterday.
He hung his head in shame as she opened the door and gave that bright sunny smile of hers.
He hugged her tight and tried to say sorry but she pulled him inside and took off his jacket, hanging it up on the beanpack rack by the door.

The Has Beans 🫘

After dinner they sat in the only two chairs her small but cozy living room contained and for the first time ever, they talked.

Really talked.

Beanardo told Beanadette about his mother, how she became an Addict and had withered away to nothing right before his eyes. He told her about life on the streets as an orphaned bean with no stalk to call his home, and her eyes filled with tears.

He told her how everybean just walked by him like he didn't exist, and how the only bean who had ever been nice to him was Mr. Beaner.

He told her how he had almost got adopted once but found out later that was a horrible place to end up, so then he decided he was thankful to be a stalkless bean after all.

"God really does know what He's doing," he said softly.

Beanadette had to agree.

Then Beanadette told Beanardo of her mother and father.
She told him she had a brother once who died after being trapped outside in the rain one stormy night. He got sick of Beanfever and never recovered.
Her parents were devastated. It took a long time to heal from the loss.
Beanardo realized Beanadette had trust issues too; she just chose to trust anyway.
He realized nobean likes to be hurt, but if a bean closes his heart off to love then he closes his heart off to life.
Beanardo and Beanadette sat and talked a long, long time. Then they prayed together.
When he left, Beanardo felt a whole lot better.

It took about two months (which is a long time by Beanland standards) but Beanardo finally learned to trust again. He also learned to share how he felt. After that, things improved a whole lot.

Beanadette was the same happy go lucky bean she always had been, but Beanardo was a whole new breed.

A weight had fallen from his shoulders he hadn't realized he'd been carrying that was way too heavy for a bean to carry in the first place.

Beanadette started to think that perhaps they did have a future, after all.

The day finally came when Beanardo decided to make a move.

He had realized he didn't want to be without Beanadette; no matter how hard life was, it was better with her in it.

He went to Mr. Beanfield's Emporium that very day.

Mr. Beanfield had all *kinds* of beanderful things in his store.

Beanardo didn't tell anybean about his new plan. Except Mr. Beaner.

The old bean nearly had a conniption fit when he saw the ring.

Beanardo was ready to catch him, just in case.

The very next Sunday Beanedette and Beanardo were taking their regular Sunday stroll in the gardens when all of a sudden Beanardo stopped. He took hold of Beanadette's hands, looked into her eyes, and said,

"All my life I've been alone. I never knew what was missing. Now I do. It's you."

Then Beanardo dropped on one knee, right there in the dirt among the azaleas, and asked her to marry him.

Beanadette had no words, but she nodded hard.

Two weeks later they were married by Pastor Greenbeans, and all their friends came to celebrate the union in true bean fashion.

Which involves all kinds of fun and games, as I'm sure you know, because you probably have beans of your own.

The Questions

Love is patient; love is kind - 1ˢᵗ Corinthians 13.4a

Do you see what life challenge this book addresses?

By the time Beanadette and Bearnardo are ready to try and work it out, why is it so hard?

Do you think our past affects our present?

Does it have to affect our future?

What are some life choices this couple have made, separately and together?

What drives or motivates their actions now?

Can a bad relationship change? Why/why not?

Do you believe the supernatural plays a part in what happens in this world? Why/why not?

Have you ever experienced anything like this in your own life?

How did you handle it? Were you successful?

ABOUT THE AUTHOR
Kari Grace was originally born in England, and is a true green bean lover.

CrossEffective Publishing, llc© 2018   All rights reserved